BAND GEEKS
GEEKS
First Chair

Calico

An Imprint of Magic Wagon
www.abdopublishing.com

by Amy Cobb
Illustrated by Anna Cattish

For Aaron, Mara, Kassidy, and Delaney—My heart, my life. Always. —AC

www.abdopublishing.com

Published by Magic Wagon, a division of ABDO, PO Box 398166, Minneapolis, Minnesota 55439. Copyright © 2015 by Abdo Consulting Group, Inc. International copyrights reserved in all countries. No part of this book may be reproduced in any form without written permission from the publisher. Calico™ is a trademark and logo of Magic Wagon.

Printed in the United States of America, North Mankato, Minnesota.
102014
012015

Written by Amy Cobb
Illustrations by Anna Cattish
Edited by Megan M. Gunderson & Bridget O'Brien
Cover and interior design by Candice Keimig

Library of Congress Cataloging-in-Publication Data

Cobb, Amy, author.
First chair / by Amy Cobb ; illustrated by Anna Cattish.
pages cm. -- (Band geeks)
Summary: Flutist Hope James is under a lot of pressure from her mother to win first chair in the band, so when Sherman Frye enrolls at Benton Bluff Junior High she panics because she knows he is better--so Hope and her friend Baylor come up with a plan to sabotage Sherman, not realizing that he is under pressure too.
ISBN 978-1-62402-074-2
1. Bands (Music)--Juvenile fiction. 2. Identity (Psychology)--Juvenile fiction. 3. Mother and child--Juvenile fiction. 4. Best friends--Juvenile fiction. 5. Friendship--Juvenile fiction. 6. Middle schools--Juvenile fiction. [1. Bands (Music)--Fiction. 2. Identity--Fiction. 3. Mother and child--Fiction. 4. Best friends--Fiction. 5. Friendship--Fiction. 6. Junior high schools--Fiction. 7. Schools--Fiction.]
I. Cattish, Anna, illustrator. II. Title.
PZ7.1.C63Fi 2015
813.6--dc23

With extra special thanks to Larry Vaught for graciously sharing his expertise and passion for music. I am forever grateful to Clelia Gore, Megan Gunderson, and Candice Keimig for taking a chance on me. —AC

2014029142

TABLE OF CONTENTS

Chapter 1
SPOTLIGHTING SHERMAN

The puck glided straight toward my goal. At the last second, I slid my mallet across the table and hit the puck. Block! It bounced against the side of the table and banked right into my opponent's goal. She never saw it coming.

"Point!" I said as the electronic score on the side of the table switched from five to six.

"Hope! How do you do that?" my best friend, Baylor Meece, asked.

"I'm not giving away all of my secrets." I smiled. One more point and I'd win. If air hockey were an Olympic sport, I'd have a wall of gold medals.

Baylor served. "So I'm getting new neighbors."

"Cool," I said, keeping my eye on the puck. One hit with my mallet sent it sliding back to Baylor.

"They have a son." She blocked it, and the puck crossed back over the centerline. "I think he's in our grade."

I hit the puck again. "Is he cute?"

Baylor set her mallet on top of the puck, stopping play.

"Errr! Foul!" I said. "You can't do that."

"That doesn't count if you want me to answer your question," Baylor said.

"Fine," I said. That foul did count. And the puck should've been mine to serve. But I didn't push it. Ever since my sister left for college, Baylor was the only person who played air hockey with me.

"Anyway, I haven't gotten a really good look at him yet," Baylor said, still hanging on to the puck. "I just know he has brown, curly hair. So maybe." She sounded hopeful.

"He's got to be better than the guy who just moved out."

"Yeah," Baylor said, nodding. "He was so gross."

"Always slobbering," I said.

"Always knocking us down."

"Always had *breath* that knocked us down," I said.

Baylor propped her elbows on the table and sighed. "I miss Cal already."

"Me too," I said.

Cal was Baylor's old neighbor's dog. The Harveys didn't have kids. So they called their overweight bulldog, Cal, their son.

They really acted like he was, too. They stuffed Cal's big gut into extra large doggie T-shirts. He even had his own closet to hang them in.

When the Harveys worked late, they paid Baylor to walk Cal to the dog park. Lots of times, I'd go with Baylor, just to hang out. Cal was a good dog. Mostly. There was this one time he lifted his leg on a toddler at the park. Not good.

"Maybe your new neighbors will have a dog," I said.

"If they do, they'll probably just have their son walk him."

"True," I said. "But you can show him the way to the dog park. If he's cute, that is."

"Hope James!" My mom knocked on my door and stuck her head in. "Have you practiced at all today? I noticed you haven't logged your time yet."

Mom keeps a practice log on the side of the fridge. I'm supposed to write down how many minutes I practice playing my flute every day. And Mom checks it. A lot. If she doesn't see numbers being logged, she bugs me. Like now.

"I've practiced," I said.

"How many minutes?" Mom asked.

I looked at my watch. "Probably thirty, so far."

"Thirty? Honey, you know that's unacceptable." Mom stood in my room now. "Unplug that air hockey table and get out your flute!"

"I will, Mom," I said. "We're just finishing our game here."

"One hundred and twenty minutes each day, Hope. You know that's how much time your sister practiced her flute to keep first chair."

"I know, Mom." How could I ever forget? Mom is constantly reminding me that Miss Perfect Mara practiced perfectly and played perfectly.

"Earning a college scholarship requires a lot of practice," Mom said.

I'm only in seventh grade. I don't think about college much yet. But no way would I tell Mom that. Besides, she thinks about it enough for both of us. So instead, I promised to practice as soon as we finished our game. That satisfied her. For now.

"Where were we?" I asked Baylor. "Oh yeah. I was just about to score another point for the win, wasn't I?" I smiled.

"Ha, ha." Baylor served. "Not this time."

We batted the puck back and forth. Baylor might be right. The more we played, the harder it was to score on her. She was getting better.

"Sherman," Baylor said, sending the puck to my side.

"Huh?" I asked.

Baylor moved to one side and made an awesome block. "His name is Sherman."

"Whose name?" I asked.

"The new boy. My neighbor," she said. "And his last name's Frye."

"Sherman Frye?" I froze.

"Yep." Baylor hit the puck hard. It slid right into my goal. "My point!" Baylor laughed and kissed her mallet.

When I didn't say anything, Baylor asked, "Hey, you didn't let me score, did you? I don't like it when somebody just gives me points."

I still didn't say anything.

"Hello?" Baylor waved her hand in my face. "Hope! Are you there, Hope?"

"*The* Sherman Frye?" I asked.

"I guess so? So what?" Baylor said.

"Game over." I unplugged the air hockey table. "That's what."

"Hey!" Baylor said, still holding her mallet. "I was making a comeback, you know."

"Sorry," I said. "But Mom's right. I really do need to practice my flute."

"Hang on. What's the big deal about Sherman Frye?"

"Remember the band workshop where kids from a bunch of different schools shadowed college musicians?" I asked.

Baylor nodded.

"Sherman was there. And he was paired with the best flutist at the college." Baylor wouldn't know because she plays clarinet. But Sherman plays flute, same as me. "Some of the other kids said that probably meant Sherman was super good."

"So why is that a big deal?" Baylor said.

"It's a big deal because he's moving next door to you. Which means he'll switch schools. Which means he'll join our band. Which means he's coming after my chair. And if I don't get first chair, then—" I closed my eyes, fell onto my bed, flopped my head over, and lolled my tongue out.

"You're dead meat," Baylor said.

I opened one eye. "Exactly."

Baylor sighed. "I don't get it. Just because your sister got a full scholarship to Grandy Gross-o Music College, I don't understand why your parents think you have to."

"It's Grandioso College of Music," I said, still playing dead. But I didn't really get it either. I mean, I'll never play flute as well as Mara. She always had first chair, and my parents expect me to get it, too. Anything less, and I would be a major disappointment to them.

"And," I came back to life then, "no first chair, no ski trip for me." I'd looked forward to our school's winter weekend trip since last year's. Going on the trip was going to be a reward from my parents for nailing my audition.

"Last year's trip was a blast," Baylor said. "You can't miss it! Remember when we got stuck on the chairlift?"

"Yeah." We were probably only stuck for a whole five minutes. Some people were scared to death up there. But Baylor and I laughed the entire time. "But if Sherman gets first chair, I'll really be stuck. At home!" I flopped back on my bed again. "I'm burnt toast."

Baylor sat beside me, twirling her long, black braid around one finger. "Maybe Sherman's not that great."

"I don't know," I said. "I've never actually heard Sherman play. I just know what the kids at the workshop said."

"People say lots of stuff, though," Baylor said. "That doesn't mean it's true. Remember when everyone at school said we were getting an awesome new player on the basketball team? Super tall, too. What did they call her?"

"Jannie Tor." I smiled. "And when she showed up, she wasn't even a new student."

"Right, instead of a new basketball player, we got a new janitor." Baylor laughed.

"And she was shorter than me!" I said.

"That's short!" She laughed again.

Baylor was right. All that stuff about Sherman could be a rumor. "I wish I knew," I said.

"Why you're so short?" Baylor joked.

"No! I wish I knew if Sherman is really that good or not."

"You'll find out when he comes to his first practice with our band," Baylor said.

"But I can't wait until then! I have to know now."

"How are you supposed to find out?" Baylor asked.

"I'm not sure." I hugged my knees to my chest.

Baylor's fingertip traced the outline of the daisies on my comforter. "Hey, I got it!"

"You do?" I sat up a little straighter.

"Yeah, we get a map of Sherman's school. We go undercover. Then we parachute into the band room. We crack the code. Mission accomplished!"

I shook my head. "What code? Have you been watching spy movies again?"

Baylor didn't say anything.

"Besides," I laughed, "last time I checked, neither one of us owns a parachute."

"True." Baylor traced more daisies.

I traced a few, too.

"I got it!" Baylor said again. "We figure out where Sherman practices, and we plant a tape recorder to record his playing." Baylor smiled. "We'll have all of the classified information we need."

"Okay, so that answers my question," I said. "You have been watching spy movies." Every time she did, she got crazy ideas.

"Hope!" Mom called from downstairs. "Practice! Now!"

"I'm on it, Mom!" I opened my case and began assembling my flute. "Sorry," I said to Baylor. "You gotta go."

"That's okay," Baylor said. "I have to write an article. And I still have to get the scoop from one of the lunch ladies about our shrinking scoops of mashed potatoes." Baylor smiled. "Get it? Get the scoop? Scoop of mashed potatoes?"

"Good one!" I smiled, too. Baylor is a reporter for our school newspaper, the *Benton Bluff Bloodhound*. And she's serious about it. I'm a *Bloodhound* photographer, so I've seen her in action. "Have fun being a PI," I said.

"Private investigator?"

"*Potato* investigator," I said, laughing.

Baylor laughed, too.

Then I said, "Hey, that's it! That's how we can find out how good Sherman really is at playing the flute."

"We'll throw mashed potatoes at him?" Baylor laughed again.

"Ha-ha. You're a reporter. Just pretend you're writing an article about him. A spotlight on the new kid," I said, lining up the foot joint of my flute.

"Great idea!" Baylor said. "We could interview kids who were in band with Sherman at his old school to see what they say about his skills. But what if we get in trouble? I haven't ever been in trouble. And I really don't want to be."

"Slow down!" I said. Baylor worries about everything—pimples, clarinet solos, choosing a nursing home when she turns ninety. She already has pamphlets. No kidding!

But anyway, the more Baylor worries, the faster she talks. It's like she was born with a built-in worry meter. "We won't get in trouble," I promised. "It's all fake."

Baylor took a deep breath. "You're right. It would be pretend." She smiled. "Let's do it!"

"Yes!" I hugged her.

"Hope James!" Mom was back at my door.

"See ya!" Baylor took off.

"I'm practicing, Mom," I said, launching into a B-flat major scale. But the whole time I practiced, I thought about our fake spotlight plan. It just might work.

Chapter 2
THE SCOOP

A couple of days later, Baylor and I met inside her top-secret detective headquarters, which was actually a tiny backyard greenhouse her mom ordered from a gardening catalog. Our first spotlight Sherman meeting began.

"Have a seat, Hope." Baylor plopped down on some bags of potting soil.

I squeezed past a wheelbarrow and sat on some bags of mulch beside her.

"So here's the scoop from my mole." Baylor perched her notebook on our desk, which was an upside-down flowerpot.

Baylor's "mole" was actually her cousin Daniel who went to Eugene Hamilton Junior High, same as Sherman had until now.

I leaned in to see the first page. Names and phone numbers were written in Baylor's neat handwriting. "Who are these people?" I asked.

"These people," Baylor said, rattling the paper, "are our informants. They've been in band with Sherman, so we'll call them up and ask them questions for our fake interview."

Baylor flipped over the page. Sherman Frye Spotlight Interviews was printed across the top. "Now we have to come up with some questions. So what do you really want to know about Sherman?" Baylor's pen hovered above the page.

"You know, how good he is at playing flute and stuff like that. I have to know who I'm up against for first chair."

"Let's start with," Baylor said as she wrote, "Number One: Tell me about Sherman Frye."

"But that's not really even a question."

"It's an old reporter trick," Baylor said. "If you ask closed-ended questions, you only get yes or no answers. It's a dead end, and you don't find out as much. But if you say tell me about this or that, people spill their guts all over the place."

"That's smart!" I smiled.

"I know! It's one of the first things I learned when I started reporting for the school paper." Baylor smiled back. "Okay, what next?" She drummed her pen against her notebook. "Number Two: What do you think about Sherman's flute skills?"

"That's good," I said. "And maybe ask them to rate Sherman's flute skills."

"Number Three: On a scale from one to ten, what would you rate Sherman's flute skills?" Baylor said as she wrote.

"Yeah, except maybe say talent, instead of skills," I suggested. "That sounds more official."

"Perfect!" Baylor agreed. "What's next?"

I shook packets of bean and squash seeds like maracas while I thought about it. "We could ask them how much Sherman practices."

"How would they know?" Baylor asked.

"Because *we* know that kind of stuff! In our band, everybody knows Zac Wiles never cracks open his saxophone case to practice at home. But everyone knows Lemuel Soriano plays the trumpet almost as many hours as he sleeps."

"That's true," Baylor said, jotting down the question for number four. "How about, Number Five: What else can you tell me about Sherman?"

I nodded. "I like that one," I said. "Do we have enough?"

"Probably," Baylor said. "But I'm going to add one more."

I watched as Baylor wrote one more. "Number Six: Is Sherman cute?" she said, laughing.

"Baylor! I'm not asking that question."

"Hey," Baylor said. "He's going to be my new neighbor, so that's important."

"Why haven't you asked me? You know I've seen Sherman around," I reminded her.

"But he's your competition. That could sway your opinion," Baylor said. "I need some unbiased opinions."

Baylor sounded just like a real reporter. "You know, you could work for a major news site someday," I said.

"Thanks!" Baylor smiled and grabbed her phone.

"Wait!" I said. "When there's no article in the paper, won't everyone find out this is all fake?" Now I was starting to worry like Baylor.

"I thought about that," Baylor said. "There's not always room to run every article, so the article gets killed. They'll probably just think that's what happened with this spotlight, too."

"Okay." Now I felt a little better about this fake article. "So who's first on our list?"

"First up is Dillan Smaltz." Baylor dialed.

"Is he answering?" I asked.

"Shh." Baylor covered the mouthpiece with her

hand. "It's ringing. And ringing. And voice mail."
Baylor hung up.

"Next is Kassidy Alderson." She held up her
phone. "Your turn!"

I took a deep breath and reached for Baylor's
phone to dial Kassidy's number. "It's ringing!"

Baylor leaned her ear closer to the phone,
listening. "Hope, she said hello!" Baylor nudged
me. "Say something!"

"Um, hi. Is this Kassidy?" I asked. "Uh, hi,
Kassidy. I'm Hope James, and, uh, I'm spotlighting
Sherman Frye as our new band member of the
month for our school newspaper."

It got easier as I went along. "Can I ask you
some questions? About Sherman, I mean."

Kassidy said yes. I gave Baylor a thumbs-up.
"Great!" I said. Then I asked Kassidy all of our
questions and wrote down her answers.

I was about to hang up when Baylor held up six
fingers and mouthed "*Number six.*"

I ignored Baylor and said, "Thank you, Kassidy!" before touching the button to end our call. Quick.

"You forgot number six," Baylor said.

I handed Baylor her phone. "Sorry, she had already hung up."

"Aw, man," Baylor said.

"But I got answers to our other questions," I said. "And it's what I was afraid of. Kassidy said Sherman has a lot of energy, and he was their best flute player. She rates him a nine out of ten. She thinks he practices more than a lot of kids. And she said he rocks at walking the dog, whatever that means."

"That's still only what one person thinks. Maybe she doesn't know what she's talking about. Don't worry, we still have three more people to call."

"Yeah, three more people to tell us how great Sherman is," I said. "It feels like my first chair is being pulled out from under me."

And I was about to fall. Hard.

Baylor and I were deciding who to call next when she got a call. The phone ringing in the quiet greenhouse made us both jump.

"It's Daniel," she said. While she listened to him, she wrote down another number. "That's awesome, cuz! Thanks so much!" Baylor hit End and then looked at me. "Guess whose number we just got."

I shrugged. "I don't know." But from the smile on Baylor's face, it had to be good.

"Sherman's band director!" Baylor squealed. "Her name is Mrs. Crafton."

"I'm not sure that's a good idea." I mean, it was one thing to call kids for our fake interview, but to bring Sherman's band director into it?

"What do you mean?" Baylor frowned. "It's better than good. It's *great*. Nobody knows Sherman's flute skills like his band director does. And," she went on, "remember what this is all about. First chair."

I nodded. "And the ski trip."

"Right," Baylor said. "I'm worried if you don't find out all you can about Sherman now to see who your competition really is, you're going to lose your chair and your trip."

"I'm worried, too," I admitted. Even though Baylor worried a lot, this time I was with her. If I wanted to keep my chair and hit the slopes, we had to find out all we could about Sherman. Even if that meant calling his band director.

"Okay, let's do it. But let's finish calling the other kids first."

Baylor nodded. "Next on our list is Olivia Nyman. I'll dial."

I watched as Baylor scribbled down notes from interviewing Olivia. Everything Olivia said lined up with what Kassidy told us, except she rated him higher—a ten! She also said Sherman was the peppiest person she knew. And at the bottom of the page, Baylor wrote "geeky cute" and drew a smiley face.

"Baylor!" I said. "I can't believe you asked that."

Baylor just smiled and handed over her phone.

It was my turn to call, and Aaron Binkley was next. I was sort of getting into this interviewing stuff. Aaron started rambling about his used reed collection, which he collected from other people in case they ever become famous. His hobby was gross and cool at the same time, but I said, "Stick with the facts, please, Aaron."

When I hung up, Baylor said, "You were awesome, Hope!" Then she high-fived me.

"Thanks! But what Aaron said about Sherman isn't so awesome. Another ten."

"It's okay," she said. "We still have Delaney Hannes left on our list." It was Baylor's turn again, so she punched in the number. "Hello! Is this Delaney?" Baylor introduced herself and began interviewing Delaney.

I pressed my ear up against the phone to listen. At first. Delaney was a real chatterbox. So while I waited for Baylor to get off the phone, I read the back of a few seed packets. I never knew overwatering carrots could cause them to crack.

"Thanks, Delaney. Bye," Baylor finally said. "Boy," she tugged on her ear when she hung up, "my ear is numb. Seriously."

"So what did she say?"

"She's a reporter for her school paper, too," Baylor said. "Makes sense. She's a talker!"

"But what did Delaney say about Sherman?" I asked.

"The same thing Kassidy did. Sherman's the best at walking the dog. Delaney even said we'd love watching him. Isn't that strange?"

"Very," I said.

"I guess with the Harveys gone, that means I'm out of a dog-walking job for sure," Baylor said.

"I'm sorry."

"That's okay," Baylor said. "Maybe I can weed the Browns' flower bed, or something."

"But what did she say about Sherman playing flute?" I asked.

Baylor shook her head. "It's not good, Hope. Delaney says she's never heard anyone play the flute like Sherman."

"That's what I was afraid of." I sighed.

"You still have to call Sherman's band director." Baylor flipped her notebook to Mrs. Crafton's phone number. "Your turn."

I touched two numbers and hung up.

"Hope, dial! You've got to hear what she says about Sherman," Baylor said.

"I know." But my mouth was dry and cottony, like I'd swallowed a gardening glove.

"Dial!" Baylor said again.

I cleared my throat and dialed. "Uh, hi, Mrs. Crafton? This is Hope James, and I'd like to ask you some questions about Sherman Frye. We're from his new school, and for our school newspaper we're spotlighting a band member of the month."

By now, I practically had my lines memorized, so at least I wasn't as nervous.

It turned out Mrs. Crafton was really nice. And informative.

"Well?" Baylor asked when I hung up.

"Mrs. Crafton said to be sure to add a quote to the article," I said. "Sherman Frye plays with fervor."

"What's fervor?"

"I have no clue, but I'm going to find out." I rested my head on Baylor's shoulder. "I'm doomed!"

"You're not doomed," Baylor said.

"I am," I said.

"No, you're not," Baylor said.

"I just wish I could hear Sherman play before chair auditions."

"Maybe you can," Baylor said.

"How?"

"He's moving in this weekend," Baylor said. "Let's go undercover."

"You mean spy on Sherman?"

"Not spy." Baylor smiled. "Investigate. That sounds nicer."

"Count me in," I said. Spy, investigate, snoop. It didn't matter what we called it. I had to know how good Sherman really was at flute. Otherwise, I was doomed. Doomed with a capital *D*.

Chapter 3
GOING UNDERCOVER

It was Saturday, and I was supposed to be at Baylor's house already to spy on Sherman. Or investigate him, as Baylor said. But Mom refused to drive me over until I practiced the entire 120 minutes she required for my practice log.

We were finally in the car headed to Baylor's, and then Mom turned off the radio. Oh no. A Mom Speech. She saves them for the car because she knows I can't escape. "Chair auditions are next week," she said in a sing-song voice.

"I *know*." She reminded me. Every. Single. Day.

Mom flipped on her turn signal and took a right on Hollan Lane, the cul-de-sac where Baylor lives. "I don't believe you're taking this seriously enough, Hope. You should spend more time practicing today. You and Baylor could always set up another play date once auditions are finished."

"It's not a play date, Mom." Play dates were for elementary school, not junior high. And I was taking auditions seriously. I was about to find out how good Sherman was. This whole day was about band, just not the way Mom intended.

"Look at Mara. Your sister practiced extra hard before auditions," Mom said. "Her chair placement reflected her diligence. She always got first."

"Saint Mara," I said. "I'm sure she'll get a golden flute at the pearly gates."

"Hope!" Mom said. "Don't be rude."

"What? It's true." Mom always compares me to Mara. But I'm not Mara.

And sometimes, I wish I didn't play flute like Mara. I wish I played something different. Like my armpit. Or spoons. Or the didgeridoo. Last year when Mr. Byrd, our band director, showed us a movie about instruments around the world, we learned the didgeridoo is a supercool wind instrument from Australia.

We pulled into Baylor's driveway then. It wasn't exactly the Outback. But for at least a few hours, I wouldn't have to hear Mom telling me how Mara's so great. And how I'm so not.

"We'll talk about this later," Mom said as I unbuckled my seat belt.

I wanted to tell her no. Forget it. But I didn't. Instead, I just said, "Bye, Mom," and climbed out of the car. I waved from the driveway as she backed onto the street.

Baylor met me there. "Where've you been?"

"Sorry I'm late. I've been practicing," I said. "Mom's orders."

"Shh!" Baylor jerked her head toward the house next door. "The suspect, aka Sherman Frye, is already on the premises."

"I'm no reporter," I whispered, "but the big green moving truck out front sort of clued me in."

Baylor linked her arm with mine. "I know Sherman's exact location. Let's mobilize!"

We sneaked past Baylor's garage and into her backyard, separated from Sherman's backyard by a wooden privacy fence.

"Base of operations for today," Baylor whispered, climbing onto the trampoline beside the fence.

When I climbed up beside her, Baylor said, "We can see straight into Sherman's yard from here." Then she handed me a green, leafy tree branch from the trampoline's edge. "Here's your cover. Wear it."

I raised an eyebrow. I wasn't sure exactly where I should wear a tree branch. So when Baylor perched her branch on her head, I did the same.

"Remember, *covert*," Baylor whispered.

"What?"

"Top secret," she said. "On three, slowly ease up to peek over the fence." She held up her fingers one by one, and we popped up for a sneaky peek.

"What'cha doin'?"

Baylor and I both screamed.

Baylor's older brother, Kennet, stood behind us, laughing. "You screamed like little girls!"

"Kennet!" Baylor yelled. "Go away!"

"What if I don't want to? I might wear leaves on my head and hang out with you today." Kennet leaned against the trampoline, in no hurry to leave.

"Please go away," Baylor said again.

"Well," Kennet pretended to think about it, "since you begged. But you owe me half of your dessert tonight."

"Done," Baylor said. When Kennet left, she said, "He doesn't know we're having blackberry cobbler tonight. And he won't eat it because the seeds stick in his braces."

"Ew!" I wrinkled my nose.

"Try sitting across the table from him." Baylor made a sound like she was sucking food from between her teeth. "Anyway, straighten your cover," she said, rearranging my leaves. "Better. Now let's try this again."

"Wait a minute." I grabbed Baylor's shoulder. "I hear someone talking."

"Is it Sherman?"

I put my ear next to the fence. "It has to be."

Baylor put her ear against the fence, too.

"Come on, boy. We're trying this trick one more time," Sherman said. "And if you don't walk right, you're a done dog."

My mouth dropped open. "Did you hear that?"

"Uh-huh." Baylor nodded, her eyes huge.

The dog must not have performed the trick because then Sherman said, "You're just too old. I'm stuffing you in a box. Off to the dump with you."

"I can't believe it," Baylor whispered.

"Me neither!" I jumped off the trampoline.

"Hope! Where are you going?"

I broke into a run. Right now, I didn't care about Sherman's flute skills. All I cared about was his dog.

Baylor was yelling after me, but I didn't stop. By the time I got to the front of Sherman's house, he was already there, sliding the truck's door closed.

"Please!" I cried. "Don't do it!"

"Huh?" Sherman whirled around.

"Just because he's old, you can't throw him away like garbage," I said, catching my breath. "I'll even help you look for another home for him."

Baylor nodded. "We both will."

"But nobody'd want that old thing," he said.

"You'd be surprised," I said. "Please, give him a chance."

"I guess we can see if anybody else wants him, if it really means that much to you," Sherman said.

"It does," I said.

When Sherman opened the truck door, I smiled at Baylor. We'd convinced him to change his mind, and it felt good to save a life today.

I looked past Sherman to the boxes still inside the truck. Hopefully Sherman's dog wasn't too big.

I'd have to take him home with me until we found him a forever home, and a smaller dog would probably go over better with Mom.

But the box Sherman pulled out was a cereal box. Sherman must be joking. He tilted it upside down and gave it a shake. An old blue yo-yo landed in his hand. "If anybody wants him, it's fine by me," Sherman said, handing it to me.

I stared at Sherman's yo-yo and its knotted, frayed string. It was past due for a one-way dump trip. "I don't get it," I said. "We heard you say 'boy' and that your dog was headed to the dump if he didn't do his tricks."

"Yeah." Sherman pulled a lime-green yo-yo from his pocket. He flicked it slightly behind him, and the yo-yo "walked" forward along the ground. "That trick is called walking the dog."

"Cool!" I said. Now I totally got why the band kids we interviewed told us Sherman rocked at walking the dog.

"Thanks!" Sherman walked the dog a few more times.

"But why did you call your yo-yo 'boy'?" Baylor asked.

"Just for fun because I can't have a real dog. I'm allergic. This one is new," he said, sticking the lime-green one back in his pocket, "but I think it's a girl." Then Sherman crossed his arms. "So why were you eavesdropping on me, anyway? Should I report you to somebody?"

I could see Baylor's worry meter spin off the charts. "Nope, we were just hanging out. You know, in my yard. On the trampoline. And we just heard. We couldn't help it. Don't tell on us." Baylor finally took a breath. "Please."

"Okay." Sherman seemed satisfied. "I thought maybe you were fangirls or something."

Fangirls? Of Sherman's? I wanted to laugh. But he gave me an idea.

"You'll probably have some fans soon, though," I said.

"I will?" Sherman stood a little straighter.

"Yeah," I said. "See, Baylor, here, is a reporter for our school newspaper."

"Your school, too, when you get moved in," Baylor chimed in.

"Since you're in band, we want to spotlight you for a band member of the month article," I said.

"Wait," Sherman said. "How did you know I'm in band?" His eyes narrowed on me. "You really are a fangirl, aren't you."

"No," I shook my head, "I'm not a fangirl." Then I added, "Yet. But I might be after your interview."

Sherman must've liked the idea because he said, "Follow me."

So we all sat on Sherman's front porch steps. "Ask away," he said, leaning against the railing.

I started the interview. "So you play flute, right?"

"Yep." Sherman smiled. "You seem to know a lot about me."

I shrugged. "You look like a flutist."

"How long have you played flute?" Baylor asked.

"Since fifth grade," he said.

So we started playing at the same time.

"On a scale of one to ten, how high would you rate yourself?" I asked.

"I'd say a—" Sherman began, then stopped. "Wait, the scale only goes to ten?"

I nodded.

"Let's just say at my old school, nobody played the flute like me. So I'm a ten-plus."

"Show us." With first chair on the line, I felt brave then. If Sherman was that good, I wanted to hear him play. Today. Right now.

"Okay," Sherman agreed. "But I have to warm up first."

This was easy. Almost too easy. Instead of warming up on his flute, Sherman ran over to a tree and did chin-ups on a lower branch. Then he waved his long arms above his head, wiggled his legs, and jiggled around like a spaghetti noodle.

Baylor looked at me. "Whoa."

"Double whoa," I said. "Sherman has tons of fervor, just like Mrs. Crafton said."

"Huh?"

"It means enthusiasm. Or excitement," I said.

Baylor raised an eyebrow.

"I looked it up!" I said.

After Sherman did jumping jacks, he said, "I'm all warmed up. I'll grab my flute."

"Sherman Frye!" The front door swung open. And it looked like Sherman's curly brown hair had been copied and pasted onto the woman in the doorway. She had to be his mom. "You can make new friends later," she said, eyeing Baylor and me. "But with chair auditions next week, there's no time for dawdling. Come inside. Now!"

"Later, fangirls," Sherman said.

"We're not—" I started. But what was the use? I'd been so close to finding out just how good Sherman's skills really were. Instead, I found out he lives with a Band Mom like mine. If Sherman wasn't my competition, we might've been friends.

Chapter 4

BEST FLUTIST FOREVER

That afternoon, I tiptoed upstairs to my room. Mom said earlier that we'd talk later, and I hoped to make it much later. I was easing my door open when Mom spotted me.

"There you are, Hope," Mom said.

"Yep. Here I am," I said. "And now I must organize my sock drawer. My no-shows got mixed up with my toe socks. And don't get me started on those ankle socks. Cuckoo!" I circled my finger around my ear. Then I backed into my room. Slowly. *Almost there. Don't look her in the eye.*

"I'm happy you're excited about cleanliness," Mom said. "But your dad and I would like to speak with you first."

Great. Tag-team lecture time.

"Look who's home, Dad," Mom said when we found him downstairs in the kitchen.

My parents call each other Mom and Dad. It probably started when Mara and I were babies, to help us learn which parent was which. Dad's beard kind of gives it away, though. And even if Mom has a little more fuzz on her chin than she used to, I'm pretty sure at this point we can still tell them apart.

Dad popped a casserole in the oven and hugged me. "How's my girl?"

"I'm fine, Dad."

"Great!" he said, pulling out a barstool. "Let the family meeting begin. Take it away, Mom."

"After this morning," she began, "I feel like you need motivation, Hope. This might help." Mom handed me a gift-wrapped box. "Open it."

I shook it. Whatever was inside slid around. But I still couldn't guess what it was. So I tore through the cupcake wrapping paper to read Sara K's on the box lid. With tons of funky jewelry and cool clothes, it is easily my favorite store. The box fit in the palm of my hand, so I guessed jewelry. When I looked inside, I saw my guess was right.

"Thank you," I said, pulling out a shiny gold bracelet. Two charms dangled from it, one a music note and the other the letters *BFF*.

"I know the letters stand for best forever friends," Mom said.

"It's best friends forever, Mom," I said.

"Well, since it has a music note," Mom went on, "at our house, *BFF* stands for best *flutist* forever." She clapped her hands. "Isn't that fun?"

I couldn't give her my honest answer.

"And look." Mom pulled out another box. "I got Mara one, too. You girls will match."

Dad put one finger to his lips. "Shh. Don't tell her. It's a secret."

"I won't," I promised, putting mine on. BFF. Best flutist forever. That sounded like something Mom would come up with. But I'd expected another Mom Speech comparing my flute skills to Mara's, so this was a really nice surprise.

I hugged Mom and Dad and thanked them again. And it seemed like the perfect time to bring up Sherman. I told them all about how he was joining our band and how good everyone said he was. I ended with, "My first chair feels wobbly. I'm afraid Sherman is going to unseat me."

I really wished for once they would just say that if that happened, it would be okay. Just to do my best. But they didn't.

Mom said, "Nobody ever beat Mara for first chair. And Sherman Frye won't beat you, either."

I'm not Mara, I wanted to scream.

"Mr. Byrd will be handing out Saturday's audition schedule this week, yes?" Mom asked.

"Yes," I repeated.

"Then you have exactly one week to prepare, so you need to dig deeper." Mom might've watched some motivational videos while I was at Baylor's because she doubled up her fists and punched the air as she said, "Really practice more."

"Yeah!" Dad left-hooked the air, too.

Did they rehearse this?

Mom grabbed her shopping list, flipped it over, and started writing on the back of it. When she was finished, she handed me her list. "I know exactly what you need," she said.

"Pickles, refried beans, prune juice," I read.

"No, read the other side," Mom said.

She'd whipped up a new practice log. "You want me to practice an extra hour? Every day?" I asked.

"Keep in mind, it's only for the next week until auditions end," Dad said. "Right, Mom?"

"Right." Mom nodded. "Adding an extra hour to your practice log only totals three hours each day."

"*Only* three hours?"

"If you're going to keep Sherman out of first chair, you simply must practice harder. Add a little time each morning before school." Mom smiled. "Wear your new bracelet for motivation!"

I looked down at my bracelet. Before, it felt light on my wrist. Now it was heavy, like a chain dangling there. A reminder to practice more, *or else*.

Chapter 5
SHERMAN SHOWS UP

I thought Sherman might not switch to my school after all. He wasn't in band all week. But no such luck. On Thursday, Sherman officially joined.

Mr. Byrd stood at the front of the band room in a straw hat and tropical shirt, the only kind he ever wore. This one bloomed with purple hibiscus flowers. He waited until everyone settled down to introduce Sherman.

"Mr. Frye is joining our woodwinds, and just in time for Saturday's chair auditions," Mr. Byrd said. "Please welcome him."

Sherman kept the purple theme going with the button-up shirt he paired with a lime green bow tie to make his band debut. He hugged his flute case to his chest and waved. When Sherman joined the rest of us flute players, he said, "Greetings, fellow flutists! Who's ready to warm up?"

"For warm-ups, we usually wait for Mr. Byrd to lead us," said Lilly Reyes, sitting beside me in second chair.

Then Sherman reached his hands high above his head and wiggled his fingers.

"What are you doing?" Lilly asked.

"Warming up," Sherman said. "I call this next move the mixer." He put his hands on his hips and bent side to side, then forward and backward. "See how I mix up my moves?"

Lilly whispered to me, "Think we can trade him to the brass section?"

I smiled. That would solve all of my first chair problems. But watching Sherman jump an imaginary jump rope, I doubted that would happen. At least I'd get to hear Sherman play his flute today, and I'd finally know if he was good. Or not.

So far, Sherman hadn't said anything to me. I started staring at my sheet music, pretending I was really interested in studying every measure. But then I felt someone tap the top of my head. *Please don't be Sherman. Please don't be—* "Sherman!" I said, glancing up. "Where've you been all week?"

"Hi, Hope!" He held his hand out to shake mine.

Ew, it was sweaty.

"We had a few things to sort out before I changed schools," Sherman said. "I didn't know you play flute, too. Why didn't you tell me when you were at my house?"

"Um, I guess I didn't think about it," I said.

"Yeah, you were too busy getting to know me better." He wiggled his bow tie. "Fangirl."

Lilly's eyebrows shot up. "You were at his house?"

"I can explain," I said. But really, I couldn't. If I did, then I'd have to spill about the article Baylor and I were pretending to write for the *Bloodhound*. And nobody could know about that. Nobody.

But I didn't have to worry about it. Mr. Byrd stood on the podium at the front of the band room. "Please assemble your instruments," he said. After a few minutes, Mr. Byrd raised his arms, ready to lead us through some real warm-ups with our instruments, not the stretches Sherman just did.

But before a single note was played, Sherman raised his hand and said, "Mr. Byrd!"

"Yes, Sherman?" Mr. Byrd said.

Sherman held up his flute. "You won't believe this. I was cleaning my flute last night, and I forgot to put my head joint back in my case."

Mr. Byrd nodded. "Take the hall pass and call your parents."

"And I forgot my neck strap," Zac added, waving his saxophone. "I need a hall pass, too."

Lilly whispered, "I hope Sherman's not forgetful like Zac."

"For real," I whispered back. Every practice began with Zac forgetting something. We were all used to him goofing off, and I was pretty sure he forgot stuff on purpose.

I didn't know Sherman that well, but I thought he'd take band more seriously. It would be good for me if he didn't, though. And for my chair.

When Sherman and Zac left, Mr. Byrd waved his baton to direct us as we played up and down scales and practiced slurs and long tones. We played some of them as a full band. For others, Mr. Byrd called out "Trumpets!" or "Clarinets!"

After that, we worked on rhythm exercises before we played a classical piece we'd just started working on. Mr. Byrd broke that down, too, and worked with individual sections.

"Now let's play that as a full band," Mr. Byrd said. "One more time!"

"You know what that means," Lilly whispered.

"Yeah." I smiled. "One more time means we're going to play it at least five more times."

Zac strutted into the room then, swinging his neck strap. I bet it was in his pocket the whole time. But Sherman still wasn't back.

Thinking about that got me behind on my timing. I sped up my tempo, trying to catch up.

Mr. Byrd cupped one hand behind his ear, listening. "Stay together! Someone's timing is off!" he said, looking at me.

I've never figured out how he does it, but Mr. Byrd can always tell who is off. He never calls anyone out, but you always know when it's you. And right now, he knew I was the off-time someone.

When the song ended, Mr. Byrd said, "One more time! And this time, play like you're on stage at Lincoln Center!"

I was wrong. We didn't play that song five more times. We played it eight more times before the end of practice.

Then came the announcement we'd been waiting for. "As you know," Mr. Byrd began, "tomorrow is Audition Eve. To de-stress, we'll watch a movie instead of playing. Auditions will be held right here." He pointed to the band room floor.

"For your audition, you'll need to know a passage from the song you just played." Mr. Byrd held up the schedules. "Grab one before you leave. Questions?"

Sherman returned then with his head joint. "Yeah, what did I miss?" he asked.

"Everything," Mr. Byrd said. "Practice is over."

"Oh, man!" Sherman said, taking a seat.

But Sherman didn't look upset. He looked almost relieved. And I wondered why.

"Practice! Practice! Practice!" That was the last thing Mr. Byrd had said to us as he passed out audition schedules. When I got home from school, I tried to practice. Seriously.

But then I thought about something else Mr. Byrd had said. We'd be watching a movie tomorrow, instead of playing our instruments, to de-stress. And I got more stressed. Tomorrow was my last chance to hear Sherman play before auditions. Now that wasn't happening.

Plus, it wouldn't even be a real movie. Mr. Byrd's "movies" are home videos his mom recorded of his high school marching band competitions.

As she filmed, his mom yelled, "That's my baby!" A lot. And when she clapped, the camera shook like she was filming an earthquake. That part was sort of fitting, though, because the uniforms Mr. Byrd's band wore back then were a total disaster.

So instead of practicing, I played air hockey by myself. And I was winning until Mom heard me.

"Hope! Turn that off! Have you practiced?"

"Mom, I just got home."

"Practice first. Games second," Mom said. "You only have two days until auditions. And speaking of auditions, let's see the schedule."

Of course we were speaking of auditions. That's all Mom ever talked about. She had Band Mom brain. But I handed her the schedule.

Mom skimmed through it to find my name. "There you are. Hope James. Two o'clock. And right after you is Sherman Frye." Mom shook her head. "I'm sure you'll follow in your sister's footsteps."

I wished I was so sure. But I wasn't. The fake article Baylor and I worked on totally bombed. And with only two days until auditions, there was zero chance of hearing Sherman play now. But then again, maybe I didn't have to. Maybe there was another way.

So I told Mom I needed to practice at Baylor's house. At first, she was against it. But then I brought up her motivation speech, and I told her playing with Baylor motivates me to practice harder. Mom finally agreed to let me go, but only for a couple of hours. That was all I needed.

When Mom dropped me off, I told Baylor my idea. "So what do you think?" I asked.

"It's worth a shot," Baylor said. "Let's go to Sherman's."

But when we knocked on the door, Sherman's mom told us he was busy preparing for chair auditions. She said we shouldn't bother him, right before she shut the door in our faces.

"Sherman's mom is like a guard dog," I said, jumping off their porch step.

"Yeah, a real Rottweiler," Baylor agreed.

We headed back to Baylor's and ended up on the swing set in her backyard. We used to race, seeing who could swing the highest. But since we'd turned twelve, we just sort of hung out, spinning in slow circles.

"So how do we get past Sherman's guard dog mom?" I asked.

"Throw her a juicy bone," Baylor joked.

"Good one!" I smiled. "Or call the dog pound."

Baylor laughed.

I kicked at a pebble. "Maybe this idea wasn't so great after all."

"At least you tried, though."

Neither of us said anything for a while after that. We sat on the swings, both of us writing our names in the dirt with the toes of our sneakers. Except for birds fluttering in the treetops, it was totally quiet. And peaceful.

Until someone grabbed our swings from behind, giving them a shake.

"Kennet!" Baylor yelled.

We both jumped up and whirled around. But it wasn't Kennet bugging us as usual. It was Sherman.

"Greetings, fangirls!" He laughed. "I didn't mean to scare you."

"It's okay," I said. Actually, it was better than okay. Now my idea might still work. "But why aren't you practicing? Your mom told us not to bug you."

"I needed a break," he said. "And I saw you from my window. It looks straight into your backyard."

"That's creepy," Baylor said. Then she joked, "Do we need to report you?"

"I come in peace!" Sherman made the peace symbol with his fingers.

But did he really? If he stole first chair from me, I'd never have any peace from Mom again. It was time to put my plan into action. I had to be honest with Sherman about chair auditions.

"You know," I jumped right in, "if I don't get first chair on Saturday, my life will not have a happy ending." Okay, dramatic maybe. But true.

Sherman didn't say anything. He obviously didn't get how serious this was.

"See, my sister owned the first chair flute position. And my mom expects me to own it, too," I explained. "So maybe you could try out for something else. The cheer squad is always looking for male cheerleaders."

Sherman nodded, like he was thinking about it.

"Chess club has openings, too," Baylor said, smiling at Sherman. "And I'm in chess club."

"Really?" Sherman smiled back.

Forget chess club. This was no time for Baylor to flirt with the enemy.

"Or you could start a yo-yo club," I said. "Your tricks are awesome."

"I'd love to do all of that stuff!" Sherman said.

"You would?" I looked at Baylor. I didn't think he'd change his mind this quickly.

"Yeah," Sherman said. "But I can't. I had first chair at my old school, and my mom really wants me to get it here, too. She's even made me up my practice time this week. Can you believe it?"

I nodded. "My mom is slamming me with extra practice, too."

"I'll just be glad when auditions are over." Sherman pulled his phone from his pocket, where it had started buzzing. "That's Mom now. Practice time. Again."

I felt sort of sorry for Sherman, even if he was my competition. I understood how he felt.

"May the best flutist win, fangirl," Sherman said. "Of course, we both know that's going to be me." Then he took off.

"Smackdown! I can't believe he said that," Baylor said.

I couldn't either. And for the rest of the night, Sherman's words were stuck in my brain. *The best flutist.* Was that Sherman? Or me?

Chapter 6
OPERATION NO-SHOW SHERMAN

Baylor met me at my locker first thing the next morning. "Hope, you'll never believe what I saw last night!"

"If it's another story about your cat's hair balls, save it. Please!" I said, ready to plug my ears.

"No, silly!" Baylor laughed. "I watched *Mysteries Magnified.*"

"Another spy show?" I asked.

"Not just a spy show," Baylor said. "*The* spy show. The show that's going to fix your band year."

I leaned against my locker. "I don't get it," I said.

"Okay, so there's Sven, the spy boss. He and the bad guys all want the hidden jewels, sort of like you and Sherman both want first chair," Baylor explained.

"But Sven switched the top secret map with a fake one to keep the bad guys from finding the jewels. See?" She smiled. "All we need is a switcheroo. And," she snapped her fingers, "no more Sherman problems."

"Gotcha. We're moving the band room somewhere else. But," I frowned, "do you think we can have everything moved before auditions tomorrow? And won't Sherman just track us down?"

"Hope," Baylor said. "You really need to watch more spy shows. The only thing we're moving is Sherman's audition date."

"What?" I asked. "How?"

"I'll debrief you at lunch," she said over the bell.

Baylor practically skipped down the hall. I headed to science, wondering what she was up to.

I grabbed my lunch tray and scanned the cafeteria. I finally found Baylor at a corner table.

"So what's up?" I asked before I even sat down.

"You." Baylor squeezed mustard onto her fries. "At least, you will be when Sherman's a no-show at auditions. And," she dunked a fry, "when you get first chair."

"I'm pretty sure Sherman'll be there," I said. Baylor had gotten my hopes up for nothing. "You heard him yesterday. His mom wants him to get first chair. And he's been practicing his guts out."

"Nope," Baylor shook her head. "Trust me. Sherman won't show up tomorrow."

I swallowed a bite of my burger. "Am I missing something here?"

"To save your chair, we're going on a special operations mission to copy the audition schedule file from Mr. Byrd's computer," Baylor said. "After we get it, we'll change the date on there."

"And then we give it to Sherman, and he won't show up at chair auditions tomorrow because he'll have the wrong date," I said, a little surprised at

Baylor. Apparently being a spy trumped her fear of getting in trouble!

"Exactly!" Baylor said.

"Baylor! You're part genius!"

"A spy genius!" She wiggled her eyebrows up and down and smiled.

"Hey, we need spy names," I said.

"Aliases! Good idea!" Baylor said. "Secret Agent James for you and Secret Agent Meece for me?"

"But that's not very top secret." If I was going to be a spy, I wanted a cool name at least.

"We could use our favorite color and our favorite class," Baylor suggested. "Agent Green Band!"

"I'd be Purple Band," I said. "They're too similar."

Baylor scrunched up her nose. "Yeah, they're practically the same. Let's pick something else."

I popped my last fry in my mouth while I thought about it. "I know!" I finally said. "Your first name is the name of your favorite pet. Your last name is what you had for breakfast this morning."

"That could work," Baylor said. "My very first fish was named Fuzzy."

"Fuzzy?" I asked.

"Hey, I was two. So I named a googly-eyed goldfish Fuzzy," she said. "And this morning, I ate waffles."

"Fuzzy Waffles!" I laughed. "That's perfect."

"Yeah, I kind of like it." Baylor smiled. "Let's figure out yours."

"Well, my favorite pet isn't actually my pet," I said. "But remember how I loved the pony at the fall festival last year?"

Baylor nodded.

"So I choose the name Prince," I said. "And I ate bacon for breakfast. So I'm Prince Bacon," I said.

Baylor used a British accent. "I'm quite pleased to meet you, Prince Bacon."

"Likewise, Fuzzy Waffles," I said, playing along. "And," I said, switching back to my real voice, "we could even name our mission." I was starting to get into this spy stuff. "Maybe Operation No-Show Sherman?"

"Perfect!" Baylor said. "Now all we have to do is copy the file and type up the letter. Everyone can keep their same audition times. All we have to do is switch the date. How does next weekend sound?"

"Let me check my calendar." I pretended to flip through some pages. "Next Saturday works for me."

"Good," Baylor said.

"There's one problem, though," I said.

"What?" Baylor asked.

"How are we supposed to copy the file?"

"It'll be easy," Baylor said. "Trust me."

I really wanted to trust Baylor. But what if we got caught? I've never been in trouble at school in my whole life. And twelve did not seem like a good age to start a life of crime.

"There's one other problem," I said.

"What now?" Baylor asked.

"I'm not sure this is a good idea."

Baylor propped her elbows on our table and said, "Close your eyes and picture yourself sitting in first chair."

I closed my eyes.

"Do you see yourself?" Baylor asked.

"I do." There I was, holding my flute. I even saw Mom and Dad smiling proudly in the background.

"Now," Baylor said, "picture Sherman running up behind you, pushing you out of your chair, and stealing it from you."

My eyes popped open. I didn't like that picture. If it were a drawing, I'd wad it up and toss it in the trash. Baylor was right. There was no other way.

"Fuzzy Waffles," I said. "Let Operation No-Show Sherman begin."

"Ten-four, Prince Bacon," Baylor said.

As usual, we had band right after lunch. But we didn't play our instruments because of the movie.

Mr. Byrd popped in one of his old high school band home videos. He pointed to himself in the middle of the screen. "See?" Mr. Byrd adjusted his glasses. "There I am, right up front, conducting."

Everyone laughed when Zac joked, "That can't be you, Byrd. That guy has hair."

"Yeah, yeah." Mr. Byrd tried to hide a smile. "Just watch the movie." Then he turned off the lights before sitting at his desk in the front of the room.

I couldn't focus. I still didn't know Baylor's plan to get the audition schedule file and change the date. Luckily, I didn't have to wait long to find out.

"C'mon, Prince Bacon," Baylor whispered, tugging on my arm.

With the lights off, it was really dark. I almost tripped over Lilly's feet. And Kori's trombone case. "Watch it! Are you trying to kill Russell?" she asked. Russell was what Kori had named her trombone.

"Sorry, Russell," I said, before following Baylor to Mr. Byrd's desk.

"Mr. Byrd," Baylor said. "Jasper's head is blocking the screen. Can we switch seats?"

Mr. Byrd nodded. But his eyes were glued to his old high school band marching their way across the TV screen.

Baylor gave me a thumbs-up sign. Then she whispered, "Now we have the catbird seat."

I wasn't exactly sure what that meant. More spy lingo, I guessed. But all we'd done was move up a few rows to the front of the room. After that, nothing happened. Nothing. We just watched the TV as a young Mr. Byrd directed kids in out-of-style band uniforms.

And now band was almost over. Operation No-Show Sherman was about to fizzle out before it even started. But then, Baylor whipped out her phone. Totally against the rules.

"What are you doing?" I whispered.

"Mr. Byrd is about to get a phone call," Baylor whispered back, dialing a number.

I couldn't hear everything she said. Something about needing to speak with Mr. Byrd, it was important, and yes, she'd hold.

Then Baylor pulled a thumb drive from her pocket. "Hang on to this."

"What's it for?" I asked.

"You'll find out," she said, handing it to me.

"Mr. Byrd, you have an urgent phone call. Come to the office please," came our school secretary's voice over the intercom speaker.

As soon as Mr. Byrd stood up, Baylor hung up her phone. After that, things started moving. Fast.

"Hope," Mr. Byrd said, "if the movie ends before I return, please turn off the TV."

"Yes, sir," I said. He trusted me. For now.

When the band room door closed behind Mr. Byrd, Baylor grabbed my hand and said, "Time to mobilize, Prince Bacon."

By mobilize, Baylor meant book it to Mr. Byrd's desk.

"It'll take five minutes for Mr. Byrd to walk to the office and back. Tops," Baylor whispered, reaching for Mr. Byrd's mouse. His computer screen lit up. "Help me look for the file."

I skimmed through the icons. And there were tons of them, so many that they almost hid Mr. Byrd's music note desktop background.

I read some of the file names. "Sheet_Music, Band_Boosters, Instrument_Repair. Hey, there it is!" I pointed. "Chair_Audition_Schedule."

"Nice work, Prince Bacon," Baylor said. "Now, be my lookout."

So far, nobody had even noticed us. Everyone still sat watching Mr. Byrd's old band video, probably hypnotized by the neon feathers that fluttered from the giant hats the band kids were wearing.

I stuck the thumb drive into the USB port. Baylor was about to click Copy when Sherman said, "What are you doing, fangirls?"

The movie had ended. And Sherman was headed straight toward us.

"Uh, we're uh . . . ," I stuttered.

"We're, um, you know, turning off the TV for Mr. Byrd," Baylor said. "He, um, asked Hope to turn it off when the movie was over. And, um, I'm helping her look for the remote." She finally took a breath.

Baylor couldn't stop talking, a dead giveaway that she was nervous. Her spy confidence was fading.

"And you need Mr. Byrd's computer to find the remote?" Sherman didn't look convinced. "I'm turning the lights on."

While Sherman went to flick the switch, Baylor clicked a few more keys on Mr. Byrd's computer.

"Operation No-Show Sherman is on," Baylor whispered, shoving the thumb drive back into her pocket.

"Mission accomplished, Fuzzy Waffles," I said.

"What did you call her?" Sherman asked. But he didn't give me time to answer. He'd spotted the TV remote on the corner of Mr. Byrd's desk. "How could you miss this?" He clicked the TV off.

Then Mr. Byrd returned. "We're almost out of time, but don't forget about chair auditions." Then he looked at his computer and scrunched up his face, like he'd noticed something was different.

Sherman looked straight at me.

The bell rang. Mr. Byrd turned back to us and said, "I'll see you all at auditions."

But he wouldn't. At least, not all of us. Sherman wouldn't be there. Baylor and I would make sure of it.

Chapter 7

FAKING A NOTE

After band, Baylor and I headed to computer lab, our last class of the day.

At our table, Baylor high-fived me. "We pulled it off!"

"You were awesome, Fuzzy Waffles!" I smacked Baylor's hand. Getting the file we needed was easy.

"Now," Baylor said, turning on a computer, "all we have to do is switch the date, print a new audition schedule, and give it to Sherman."

I scooted my chair closer to Baylor's, peering over her shoulder as she stuck the thumb drive into the USB port. I waited, but nothing happened. No "Chair_Audition_Schedule" file popped up. "What's wrong with it?" I asked.

"I'm not sure," Baylor said.

But we didn't have time to figure it out because Mr. Kaminski, our computer teacher, walked in and told us to turn off the computers. "Surprise!" he said. "Pop quiz!"

"This is a surprise, all right," I said to Baylor. And I wasn't talking about the quiz.

"Shh!" Mr. Kaminski said. "No talking until everyone has finished taking the quiz."

I hoped that wouldn't take too long. Baylor and I had to figure out what was going on with the thumb drive.

I finished my quiz in no time and handed it in to Mr. Kaminski. Baylor did, too. But we still couldn't check out the file until everyone finished. Then Mr. Kaminski talked about building a class website. So there wasn't much time left at the end of class.

Baylor fumbled around, trying to insert the thumb drive into the USB port one more time.

"Hurry!" I said, crossing my fingers.

"There it is," Baylor said. "Whew!"

"Maybe the computer just didn't read it before."

Baylor clicked on the file. But when it opened, we still had a major problem. It was last year's schedule! The names were all wrong and the formatting was different.

"Now what are we going to do?" I asked.

"I don't know," Baylor said.

"There's not enough time to go back to the band room to look for the right file," I said. "And even if we could, I wouldn't want to. I mean, I feel sort of bad that we did it the first time."

"Yeah, me too," Baylor agreed.

Even though we couldn't use the schedule we'd copied from Mr. Byrd's computer now, it still felt like we'd trespassed, or something.

"Any other ideas?" I asked.

Baylor shook her head.

"Me neither," I sighed. Then I sat there staring at the audition schedule in front of me. "Whatever we decide to do, we have to do it quick," I said. "Auditions begin at eight o'clock in the morning, starting with Ivy White."

Baylor leaned over to see the schedule. Then she whirled around in her seat. "Hope, you're part genius, too!"

"I am?"

"Yep," she said. "You just said Ivy White."

I thought Baylor might've really lost it this time. "What's so great about that?"

"Ivy White. Wite-Out. Get it?" she said. "We'll Wite-Out tomorrow's date and then just write next Saturday's date there instead."

"Yeah," I said. "But wouldn't that just look like a typo? And Mr. Byrd doesn't make typos. Ever."

"But Sherman doesn't know that."

"You might be on to something here," I said.

"What?" Baylor asked.

"I can type a note that says the audition date has to be changed. For, you know, like, unforeseen circumstances. People use that excuse all the time. And you could give the fake note to Sherman."

"That could work, especially since Mr. Byrd got that urgent phone call this afternoon," Baylor said.

"Exactly," I agreed.

So before the bell rang, I typed a note:

> Dear Students,
> Due to unforeseen circumstances, chair auditions will be held next Saturday. I apologize for any inconvenience.
> Sincerely,
> Elliot J. Byrd, Band Director
> Benton Bluff Junior High

"Is his middle initial *J*?" Baylor asked.

"I think so," I said. "Or is it *L*?"

"It doesn't matter." Baylor hit print. "I'm sure Sherman doesn't know Mr. Byrd's initial either."

I grabbed the note off the printer and Baylor slipped it inside her backpack. Now she could just walk next door and give it to Sherman after school.

The bell rang, and Baylor and I headed to our lockers. "Do you think Sherman will be a no-show tomorrow?" I asked, turning my lock.

"I'm not totally sure," Baylor said. "But why wouldn't he believe us?"

"You're right. Why wouldn't he?" I said.

I didn't have to worry about Sherman anymore. Tomorrow, first chair would be mine.

Chapter 8

ABANDON THE MISSION!

By the next morning, I'd changed my mind. It was the day of auditions. The day first chair flute could be mine. But I couldn't go through with our plan for Baylor to give Sherman the fake note.

I glanced at the clock on my nightstand. It was only seven thirty. Auditions hadn't even started yet. Baylor was supposed to call me last night when she gave Sherman the note. So far, she hadn't called. So maybe there was time to stop our plan.

I called Baylor, and I must've woken her up. Her voice sounded all gravelly, like "Hello?" had been her first word of the day. Perfect. She hadn't had time to give Sherman our note yet.

"Fuzzy Waffles," I said. "Please abandon Operation No-Show Sherman. I repeat, please abandon the mission. We can't go through with it. It's just not fair."

Baylor yawned. "What are you talking about, Hope? Our operation can't be abandoned."

"Yes, it can," I said. "It's early. There's still time."

"No, I mean, it really can't be canceled. I gave Sherman the note already," Baylor said.

"When?" Maybe I hadn't woken her up after all.

"Last night." Baylor yawned again.

"Last night?" I said. "But you were supposed to call me when you gave Sherman the note!"

Silence.

"Baylor, are you there?" I asked.

"Sorry! I forgot to call you."

Oh no.

"What's the big deal, Hope? I thought you wanted me to give Sherman the note," Baylor said.

"I did. But now I don't. It's the freedom to change my mind law. It's somewhere in the Bill of Rights. Or the Constitution? I get them mixed up," I joked.

But really, this was no joke. It was serious. And sort of complicated. Maybe Sherman had been a little mean, always bragging about how he played flute better than me. But if I didn't win first chair fair and square, then I didn't want it.

"I've practiced so much my fingers can practically play by themselves. And if Sherman's still better than me, there's nothing I can do about it anyway. Right?" I said.

"But, your mom," Baylor said. "Won't she explode into a million pieces if you're not first chair?"

"I can live with being a major disappointment to Mom." It wouldn't be easy, but I could do it. What I can't live with is disappointing myself. "We have to change our mission from Operation No-Show Sherman to Operation Show-Up Sherman."

"But how do we do that?" Baylor asked.

"Go to Sherman's house. Tell him the note was a joke and that auditions really are today," I said.

"Got it!"

Then Mom knocked on my door. "Hope, practice your music before we leave."

"Gotta go, Fuzzy Waffles!" I said. "Call me back and tell me what happened. Don't forget this time!"

"I won't," Baylor yawned.

Three hours later, I'd smacked the air hockey puck around a few times. I had practiced until all of the notes blurred into one giant musical blob. But I still hadn't heard from Baylor.

I couldn't take it anymore, so I dialed Baylor's number. "What did Sherman say?" I asked when she answered.

"Hope!" Baylor said. "I had this crazy dream that you called and said you'd changed your mind about giving Sherman the note."

When I didn't say anything, Baylor said, "You wanted me to go next door to tell him the truth." She laughed. "And you were wearing this ugly orange and yellow polka dot sweater. So weird!"

"Baylor! That wasn't a dream. It was for real."

I looked down at my green sweatshirt. "At least, everything but the polka dots was for real."

"Oh, thank goodness!" Baylor said. "I would never let you wear something like that."

"You fell asleep right after I called, didn't you?"

"Yep," Baylor said. "I stayed up late practicing last night. And then I watched *The Making of Mysteries Magnified*. Sorry!"

"It's okay." I took a deep breath. "Sherman's audition is right after mine. And Mom said we'll pick you up early. So we'll catch Sherman at home then. And we can fix everything."

We were giving Baylor a ride to school. And Mom always liked to arrive extra early for auditions. She said it helped me tap into my positive energy reserves, whatever that meant.

But when Mom and I stopped by Baylor's house, no one was home at Sherman's house.

Operation No-Show Sherman had worked. But it had worked too well. Now Baylor and I couldn't undo it. No matter how much we wanted to.

Chapter 9

BOOK 'EM!

Mr. Byrd didn't like students hanging around by the band room during auditions. So everyone waited in the gym down the hall.

Some kids shot hoops to pass the time. Some studied their sheet music one last time. The rest of us just hung out on the bleachers.

Baylor and I were trying to decide what the water stain on the ceiling directly above us looked like most. I said the Statue of Liberty. Baylor said a tennis racket. A leaky roof wasn't the most exciting thing we'd ever talked about, but it took our minds off of auditions. And off of Sherman missing them because of us.

But then, no joke, Mom hopped onto the hardwood floor in front of us. "I know many of you are nervous, and I'd like to share some helpful exercises to release the negative energy bottled inside you," she announced. "Everyone, please stand up."

Baylor looked at me.

I wanted to roll my eyes, but people actually listened to her. Other kids and parents got to their feet.

"Hope!" Mom motioned for me to stand, too.

As I did, Mom said, "The negative energy is on a rope. It's anchored inside your stomach. Tug on the rope." Mom put her hands to her stomach then, pretending to hold a rope that she was pulling from her guts. "Gently. Slowly."

"Dude, there's more than a rope in my stomach," Jasper Fava said. And he took off to the restroom.

That didn't stop Mom. "Close your eyes," she said. "The negativity is fading."

"So is her mind," Zac said, turning around to smile from the bleacher in front of me.

I wanted to stop then. Mom was too embarrassing. But I glanced at Baylor. Her eyes were closed. She pulled at her shirt like she really had a rope inside there. Lilly was on the other side of me. She was really getting into it, too.

So I pulled on my imaginary rope again. But negative energy didn't ooze out of me. I wasn't doing it right. I pulled harder. And faster. And spun around in circles. But then my pretend rope got tangled around my ankles. I lost my balance and wobbled right into Lilly. She lost her balance, too.

To keep from falling down, both of us tried to grab hold of something. Anything. And we both grabbed Zac in front of us. It looked like a group hug, with Zac sandwiched in the middle.

"Ladies, please!" Zac said, smiling. "Don't fight over me."

"Never!" Lilly said.

And I said, "Yeah right!" My face heated up as I regained my balance and smoothed down the dumb skirt Mom had insisted I wear. "Dress for success," she'd said. But if I'd fallen and flashed my undies just now, it would've been more like "dress for disaster" or "dress for extreme embarrassment."

By then, Mom was talking about positive vibes. But I didn't have to stick around for that part.

A high school volunteer wearing a Hello, My Name Is: Dakari sticker was helping out with auditions. He popped his head inside the gym and called my name.

I grabbed my flute case and sheet music.

"Woo! Go, Hope!" Mom's cheers floated behind me. She acted like I'd already won first chair.

Dakari held the band room door open for me. "Good luck," he said.

"Thanks. I need it."

But that probably wasn't true. Not since Sherman wasn't here, anyway. After Sherman, Lilly was my only real competition. But she didn't want my chair. She was happy in second.

My dress shoes, also Mom's idea, clip-clopped across the band room floor, all the way to Mr. Byrd's desk. A couple of other high school band volunteers sat near him.

"Hello, Hope," Mr. Byrd said. "Ready?"

"Yes, sir." I arranged my music on the stand in front of me. My hands were shaking, and a page fluttered from the stand.

"Don't be nervous, Hope," Mr. Byrd said.

That was easy for him to say. He didn't have to ride home with Mom. Or live with her until he turned eighteen. I did!

"I'm ready," I said, positioning my flute.

Mr. Byrd smiled. "Play like the musician you are!" He said that every day at practice.

So I pretended like this audition was like any regular practice. I pictured Lilly beside me in the flute section. And Baylor a few chairs down with the rest of the clarinets. And Jasper tapping on his snare drum when he wasn't supposed to.

I took a few deep breaths and began. At first, I was sort of hesitant. But by the second measure, my confidence was there. I'd practiced. A lot! My fingers flew over the keys. I nailed my song.

Mr. Byrd scribbled some notes on the sheet of paper in front of him—my score sheet. Afterward, he asked me to play a B-flat major scale. And I had to sight-read a piece of music I wasn't familiar with. Mr. Byrd nodded and smiled as I played, so I thought I did really well with that, too.

"Thank you, Hope," Mr. Byrd said. "Immediately following auditions, chair placement will be posted on the band room door." He turned to the teenager beside him. "Who's next?"

"Sherman Frye," the girl answered.

Mr. Byrd stood up. "I need to stretch my legs," he said. "I'll walk out with Hope to get Sherman."

Sherman. I'd almost forgotten about him. When Sherman wasn't out there waiting to audition, Mr. Byrd would be surprised.

Mr. Byrd whistled as we walked down the hall to the gym. But he stopped when Dakari met us at the door.

"Mr. Byrd," Dakari said, "Sherman Frye isn't here."

Mr. Byrd glanced at his watch. "Let's give him a few minutes before moving on to the next student."

Baylor came bounding out of the gym. "How'd you do?"

I shrugged, not wanting to say I nailed my audition with Mr. Byrd standing right there. "I'm thirsty," I said. "Wanna go with me upstairs to the vending machine?"

"Sure," Baylor said. Then she talked about Lilly's audition on the way up. "She thinks she did well."

"I'm glad," I said. That meant Lilly would get second chair, just like last year. Then maybe Lilly and I could catch up. We used to hang out more. Lately, Lilly was always busy. She never really said what she was busy doing, though.

When we were on the second floor, Baylor said, "Spill it, Hope! Did you get first chair again?"

I smiled. "I'm pretty sure—" I froze right outside of the library.

"Hope?"

I didn't say anything.

"Are you okay?" Baylor asked.

"Yeah, I just thought I saw Sherman in there." I shook my head, erasing the image from my mind.

"It's nerves," Baylor said. "I saw it on a TV show. Bananas made one lady nervous. And she saw them everywhere. I don't want to scare you, Hope, but that's probably what's happening to you, too."

I squeezed my eyes shut. Tight. Was I like the banana lady? Would I see Sherman's face everywhere? Swimming in my cereal bowl? In the pages of my history book? I shivered.

"Don't worry." Baylor patted my shoulder. "I watched the whole show. If it happens again, I can probably help you."

That made me feel better. We grabbed a couple of water bottles from the vending machine and headed back downstairs. But when we got there, Mr. Byrd still stood at the other end of the hall.

"Shouldn't he be auditioning someone else already?" I asked.

"Maybe the rest of us were so good, he doesn't have to hear anyone else play," Baylor joked.

But then I stopped dead in my tracks and grabbed Baylor's arm. "It's happening again."

"Huh?" Baylor asked.

"It's him," I said. "I see Sherman." Great. I'd probably end up on TV with the banana lady.

"Where?"

"Right there." I pointed. "With his mom and Mr. Byrd and my mom."

"Hope," Baylor whispered. "It's happening to me, too."

"It is?"

"Uh-huh. I see Sherman, too," Baylor said.

We looked at each other.

"There they are," Sherman said. "Book 'em!"

"Hang on, Sherman," Mr. Byrd said. "Come over here, girls." He motioned to us. "We need to talk."

Talking meant Mr. Byrd, Baylor, Sherman, his mom, my mom, and I all gathered in the band room.

Sherman handed Mr. Byrd a letter and said, "Baylor gave this to me yesterday."

After Mr. Byrd read it, he said, "First, I assure you that I never changed the audition date. Secondly, my middle initial is *I*, not *J*." He held up the letter. "Have you girls seen this before?"

Silence.

"Did you give this to Sherman?" Mr. Byrd asked.

Baylor's worry meter spun out of control. "I'm guilty. Am I in trouble? Will this go on my permanent record? I'm too young to have a mug shot!"

"Calm down," Mr. Byrd said. "Nobody is getting a mug shot today. But I would like to hear the truth."

"It's not Baylor's fault, Mr. Byrd." I swallowed. Hard. "It was all my idea." And then I spilled my guts. I came clean about the fake article and the letter. All our plans. "We wanted to tell Sherman the truth this morning, so he wouldn't miss auditions," I said. "But he wasn't home."

"That's because I took your advice about joining other clubs," Sherman said. "I started a yo-yo club."

"You did?" I asked.

"Yep," Sherman said. "Our very first meeting was today up in the library."

"So you really were in the library?" I said. "I thought I was seeing things!" That was a relief.

"I saw you, too," Sherman said. "I thought you'd both showed up for yo-yo club. But when you didn't, I decided to see what you were up to. So I came downstairs and found out chair auditions hadn't been changed after all."

"I'm really sorry, Sherman," I said.

"Me too," Baylor said.

"It's okay. But I've got my eye on you, fangirls." Sherman pointed at his eyes and then at us.

"Don't worry," I said. "It'll never happen again."

Mr. Byrd cleared his throat. "I'm glad to hear that, Hope. But I'm both surprised and disappointed in your behavior. And I hope you understand that there must be consequences." He sighed. "Regardless of your chair placement, I'd planned on assigning you the role of section leader."

"Seriously? Me, section leader?" Mr. Byrd only chose the best students to lead their sections.

"But," Mr. Byrd continued, "based on your actions, I'm sorry to say that I must now reconsider."

"Oh." I nodded. I could already picture myself as section leader, but I understood why there was no chance I'd get it now. "I'm sorry I let you down, Mr. Byrd. Believe me, I feel horrible."

"Apology accepted," Mr. Byrd said. "But I expect you to learn from your mistake, Hope."

"Yes, sir," I said.

"Hope," Mom said then, "this isn't like you. Why on earth would you do something like this?"

"Because of you, Mom." I decided to come clean about that, too.

"I don't understand." Mom rubbed her temples.

I took a deep breath. "It's too much pressure. You're always reminding me that Mara had first chair. But I'm not Mara." I held up my arm, and the BFF charm dangled from my bracelet. "And I'm not the best flutist forever. I'm more like the biggest flutist flop."

"Honey," Mom began. "You're not a flop. And I'm so sorry. I had no idea you felt this way. You know I worked to pay my way through college. I wanted things to be easier for your sister and for you." She put her arm around me. "I thought a future band scholarship would make your life easier. I didn't realize I was making it harder."

I nodded. "It got worse when Sherman was always telling me he was better than me. And when we interviewed the kids at his old school, they all talked about him being the best flutist in the band. I was scared I'd disappoint you."

"I'm so sorry," Mom said again.

"I was trying to scare you so you'd think I was better than you," Sherman jumped in. "The band at my old school was small. There were only two other flutes, and they were both beginners. That's why everyone said I was the best."

"Sherman—" his mom said.

"Hang on, Mom," Sherman said. "I know you wanted me to be the best here, too. But this band is bigger, and I'm just not. So I pretended I forgot my head joint this week so I wouldn't have to play."

Sherman's mom looked surprised. "I'm sorry I put so much pressure on you, Sherman."

"It's okay," Sherman said. "Just don't do it again. I've got my eye on you, too." He raised an eyebrow.

We all laughed. And everything was starting to feel okay again. Well, almost everything.

Chapter 10

MUSICAL CHAIRS

I went to get my flute case. "Here," I said, handing it to Sherman.

"Why are you giving this to me?" he asked.

"You practiced a bunch, so you should audition." I looked at Mr. Byrd. "If it's not too late."

Mr. Byrd smiled. "I can fit you in."

Sherman looked nervous now.

"You'll do fine," Mr. Byrd said. "Just play like the musician you are."

After Sherman's audition, three other students went. Annastacy Timms was last. When she finished her audition, she walked into the gym and said, "Mr. Byrd said chair results will be posted on the band room door in thirty minutes." Her eyes were kind of wide. Mine probably looked the same.

Half an hour. Then I would finally know. It was hard to wait. But I thought of a way to help time pass faster.

"Hey, Sherman," I said. "Do you have your yo-yo with you?"

He pulled it from his pocket. "Always."

"Can you show us some tricks while we wait?" I asked.

"Sure," he said.

"Yo-yos," Zac laughed. "Talk about geeky."

But when Sherman walked the dog, Zac wasn't laughing. "Cool!" Zac said. "How'd you do that?"

"It's easy," Sherman said. And he did it again.

"What else can you do?" I asked.

Sherman held his yo-yo sideways and tossed it to the side. With his left hand, he ran his fingers down the string toward the yo-yo while it spun. Then Sherman tossed it up, and the yo-yo shot straight across to his right hand. "That's the UFO," he said.

"Awesome!" Baylor said.

"Can you teach me a trick?" I asked.

"Sure. The gravity pull is an easy place to start," he said.

Sherman showed me where to put the string on my middle finger and how to hold the yo-yo in my palm for it to roll right off my hand.

"Now act like you're making a muscle to toss the yo-yo," Sherman said.

"I don't have to act." I flexed my muscles. "Check 'em out," I joked.

"You must have magic muscles. They've disappeared." Sherman smiled.

"Very funny." I said, but I smiled back.

It took a few tries, but I finally got the hang of turning my hand over and bouncing the yo-yo back up.

"Hey, I did it!" I said. "Can I join your club?"

"Hmm . . ." Sherman crossed his arms and pretended to think about it. "Sure, why not?"

And I wasn't the only one who wanted to learn yo-yo tricks. Baylor gave it a try. Zac did, too.

By the time Mr. Byrd announced that chair results were posted, Lilly had joined the club, too.

"Lilly! Now we can hang out in band *and* yo-yo club. I've missed you lately," I said on our way to the band room.

Lilly smiled. "I've been practicing a lot for chair auditions. Way more than I did last year, even."

"That's great," I said. But I hoped she wouldn't be mad when she got second chair and I got first. I mean, second chair was still really good.

Everybody wanted to be the first to read the list posted on the band room door. Baylor was lost somewhere in the crowd. Lilly and I stood in the back of the line together, slowly inching closer to the front. Some kids cheered, excited about the chairs they'd gotten. Others fought back tears because they hadn't done as well as they'd hoped.

"I can't believe it!" Baylor squealed.

She skipped toward me. "I got first chair clarinet! I never thought that would happen!"

We jumped up and down. "Congratulations! Ski trip, here we come!"

Baylor got this funny look on her face. "Um, well, you know, skiing isn't that fun. Not really. I mean, the snow is really cold. And, um, it's frozen. And cold," she said again. "Brrrrr!"

"Yeah," I said. "That's snow. Cold. And frozen."

Baylor giggled. The same way she does when she's nervous about playing a solo. And she was talking fast. I knew her too well. Something was up.

It finally cleared out enough for Lilly and I to find our last names listed in alphabetical order on the sheet. I skimmed down to *H*. And there I was, right below Ava Iskowitz.

But the names all sort of blurred together. At first, I thought I'd read the results wrong. I put my finger on my name and followed it over to the results column again. Nothing changed. Hope

James. Second Chair. That explained why Baylor was acting strange. She'd seen it, too.

And Baylor knew without first chair, I wouldn't be going on the ski trip.

Then I noticed tears on Lilly's cheeks. "Are you okay?" I asked. I hadn't even checked anybody else's placement. Had Sherman gotten first, bumping Lilly all the way to third chair?

Lilly smiled. "I'm better than okay," she choked out. "I got first chair!"

"Wow, Lilly!" I said. "Congrats!"

She stopped smiling then and just looked worried. "I hope you're not mad."

"No, I'm really happy for you, Lilly. Seriously. And we still get to be stand partners." And I meant it. I mean, of course I had hoped I would get first chair. That's all I'd thought about lately. And I'd practiced like crazy. But Lilly had told me how hard she'd practiced, too. So she earned it. And I earned second.

I got Mom's attention across the hall and held up two fingers to let her know I got second chair. She actually smiled and gave me a thumbs-up, which felt amazing.

Sherman walked over then to see what chair he got. "Hey," he said, "I got third chair! That's better than I thought I'd do." He smiled. "How about you, Hope?"

"I got second." It was sort of hard to say at first, but it was getting easier.

"First, second, and third." Sherman pointed to Lilly, to me, and then to himself.

"But it's sort of like musical chairs," I said. "Next year, it can change."

"So don't either of you get comfy. Next year, I'm coming for your chairs," Sherman joked.

"Bring it, Sherman!" I laughed. "You can have mine, but I'm going for Lilly's."

"You're both going down!" Lilly laughed, too. "I'm hanging on to this one!"

Before, I thought if I lost first chair, I lost everything. But I was wrong. I hadn't lost anything. Instead, I'd gained Sherman as a friend. And I'd showed Mom it was okay if I wasn't *the* best, as long as I was *my* best. From where I sat, the view from the second chair looked pretty great.